Emily

By
Charlotte Gingras

Illustrations by
Stéphane Jorisch

Translated by Susan Ouriou

ANNICK PRESS

TORONTO + NEW YORK + VANCOUVER

Text © 2005 Charlotte Gingras
Illustrations © 2005 Stéphane Jorisch
Translation © 2005 Susan Ouriou

Annick Press Ltd.
First published by Les éditions de la courte échelle inc., Montreal, Canada, as *La boîte à bonheur*. Translated from a revised version of the original French.

We acknowledge the support of the Canada Council for the Arts, the Ontario Arts Council, and the Government of Canada through the Book Publishing Industry Development Program (BPIDP) for our publishing activities.

Copy edited by Elizabeth McLean
Cover and interior design by Irvin Cheung/iCheung Design

The text was typeset in ITC Century and Fontesque

Cataloging in Publication
Gingras, Charlotte, 1943–
[Boîte à bonheur. English]
    Emily's piano / by Charlotte Gingras ; translated by Susan Ouriou ; illustrated by Stéphane Jorisch.

Translation of La boîte à bonheur.
ISBN 1-55037-913-5 (bound).—ISBN 1-55037-912-7 (pbk.)

    I. Jorisch, Stéphane II. Ouriou, Susan III. Title. IV. Title: Boîte à bonheur. English.
PS8563.I598B6413 2005   jC843'.54   C2005-903500-5

Printed and bound in Canada

Published in the U.S.A. by	Distributed in Canada by:	Distributed in the U.S.A. by:
Annick Press (U.S.) Ltd.	Firefly Books Ltd.	Firefly Books (U.S.) Inc.
	66 Leek Crescent	P.O. Box 1338
	Richmond Hill, ON	Ellicott Station
	L4B 1H1	Buffalo, NY 14205

Visit our website at: www.annickpress.com

Contents

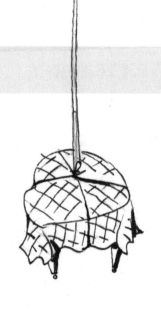

Our mother cried

The piano is gone. The flowered couch, too. And my parents' bed. We've gone in one direction, my grandma in another. It's a terrible monstrous move. The day before, I heard my father say to my mom, in a voice not to be argued with, "We'll sell the piano and some of the furniture. There won't be enough room in the new apartment."

It's true the piano was out of tune, abandoned at the back of the long living room. No one had played it for years. I was the only one who still visited it, stroking its sides, sitting under its belly to read or daydream.

In our home, we didn't celebrate Christmas or birthdays anymore. There was so much empty space, even with my grandma shut in her bedroom, that I could hear my steps echo in the hallway.

I didn't get to see the move. That day, one of

my big sisters babysat me at her place and forced me to play with my whining nephew. "Emily," she ordered, "pick up the baby's toys. Emily, change the baby's diaper." I stood with my arms crossed, without moving, or speaking. My twin sisters treat me like their servant.

The next Sunday, my other sister said to her twin, "Wasn't it strange the way our mother cried when they took away the piano?" Of course she cried! My sisters are so clueless. They never understand anything.

I still wonder how the movers managed to get the piano out of the apartment. The front door wouldn't have been wide enough. Maybe they took it through the dining room window. But then, how did they get it down the winding staircase?

I miss our piano.

My hand hurt

Now we live in a two-bedroom apartment. My mom and I sleep in the bedroom next to the kitchen in one of the twin beds my sisters used to sleep in. The twins left home first, long before the rest of us, to get married to men with mustaches and make crying babies.

My father sleeps all alone in my grandma's old bed in the front bedroom. My grandma—who left at the same time as the couch, the piano, and my parents' big bed—lives in a nursing home now. One of my sisters said to her twin, "That's not a home, that's where they send old people to die."

I never visit my grandma. She doesn't remember who I am. Even before, when she lived with us in the big apartment, I hardly ever talked to her and I never sat on her lap anymore. I didn't like the way she smelled. The last little while, my mom kept

complaining about my grandma's bedwetting and the danger of her smoking in bed at night now that she no longer had all her wits about her.

As for my ghost of a father, he only comes home late at night. He's in love with a woman he works with. I know because my mom and I were walking downtown one Sunday not long ago and my mom suddenly went pale. She started chasing after a car that was stopped at a red light down the street. My father's car. He was at the steering wheel and a woman sat next to him. They were talking and smiling. Yes. Smiling.

Grown-ups think I don't understand anything. They're wrong. I watch soap operas just like everyone else. What's more, I have hypersensitive ears and piercing eyes. Even my sense of smell is much better than most people's. I'd make a great bloodhound.

But that Sunday downtown, my mom wasn't able to catch up to the car in time. The traffic light turned green and the car disappeared around the corner. So she stopped in her tracks, came back

to where I stood, squeezed my hand hard in hers, and said, "Keep walking."

Since I'd recognized the woman, I figured it all out. I know a lot about life because of TV and my sisters' gossiping. My hand hurt.

About to collapse

We'd barely moved into the new apartment when my mom started going from one room to the next carrying a can of gold paint and her artist's paintbrush. She walks around looking for objects she can paint gold. Like twisted wooden lamp bases or picture frames. Or our little plaster Buddha.

The other day, she found a branch lying on the ground under the maple tree. She brought it back to the apartment and grabbed her can of paint. She painted the main bough and all the small branches, then hung glass balls on each one and stuck the whole thing in a flowerpot crammed full with stones. I had to groan when I first spotted the ugly thing sitting in a corner of the living room. A dead branch for a Christmas tree leaves a lot to be desired. Besides which, it's only the beginning of November.

Whenever my big sisters visit and see all the gold-decorated objects scattered throughout the house, they make fun of our mother behind her back. They say she's out of her mind.

Sometimes my mom passes me and runs a distracted hand through my hair, "Emily, are you all right?"

"No," I say with a smile. "I think I'm going to throw myself out the window."

"Oh, that's nice, treasure."

She continues on her way, the paintbrush in her other hand, a blank look in her eyes. Liquid gold drips onto the floor.

My mom isn't out of her mind. She's just sad. Which explains the whole gold thing. People slap on a bit of gold to help them pretend they're as happy as princes. Here in this apartment, no one is happy. I'm not even sure those twin sisters of mine are happy. Their voices don't sound cheerful. Sometimes they sound downright mean when they say things like our mom can't keep her man. As though a man were kept on a leash.

One sister says it didn't help matters any when I was born ten years ago. Even though, at the time, the doctor told our mother it would be good for her to have a baby to look after.

An evil curse seems to be hanging over us. Ever since the piano disappeared, it seems as if everything has been getting worse—our family is leaking, cracking, and shaking all over as though it were about to collapse.

As the world shrinks

I hate sleeping in a bed so close to my mom's bed. There's barely enough room to walk between them. The space is so narrow you have to turn sideways to shuffle through.

Big boxes full of picture albums and music books, fancy gloves, scarves, concert programs, and costume jewelry cover the whole top shelf and the back of the bedroom closet. My mom's clothes and mine are on hangers packed together tightly. Sometimes at night, when my mom's asleep and I lie waiting for her whistling breath beside me, it feels as if the world is shrinking and about to smother me.

My father caught the flu recently so he had to stay at home in the front bedroom for a couple of days. My mom picked fights with him and made him swallow bitter pills and seaweed broth.

There's no hope of a truce in this family now. We criticize each other, we tell each other's secrets. Sometimes we scream insults.

I know that the sadness and feeling of being abandoned are what's behind the cans of gold paint, the fights, the twin-bedded bedroom, our grandma in a nursing home, and our piano that's gone who knows where. I'm sure the piano is with some family in a big house and a huge living room with a chandelier. An urgent call has been put out for a piano tuner. I can picture him hitting the A key over and over again, holding his tuning fork to his ear.

My mean-mouthed sisters

My sisters and their families sometimes come for Sunday brunch. My father always brings out a cigar to chew on after the meal. His cigar makes me sick. He only stays home on the Sundays my sisters come with their husbands and their crying babies. I guess his other woman must be busy those days. He likes talking politics with his sons-in-law or playing horsie with his grandchildren on his knee. "Giddy-up, giddy-up," he cries, clicking his tongue and blowing smoke in their faces.

My mom yells at him for poisoning the grandchildren, making the living room drapes smell all smoky, and turning the new paint on the walls yellow. Sometimes she shuts herself in the twin-bedded bedroom. Or she rattles pots and pans in the kitchen. I worry about my mom.

On those Sundays, my sisters try to bribe me to take their runny-nosed brats outside to play, but I always turn them down. Well, what are fathers for? Sometimes one of the dads will stand up with a sigh, pick up his kid, put on his outdoor clothes, and go out for a walk.

I stay in the living room cluttered with gold objects and the Christmas bough in its flowerpot. I try to hear what my twin sisters are busy whispering to each other.

They say the reason our mother lost our father is that she's always in a bad mood. They talk about how pretty the other woman is.

I think my big sisters are mean. As for their husbands, I would never have married them myself. Anyhow, I keep eaves-dropping on my sisters.

Then, last Sunday, I heard one of my sisters say to her twin, "In the old days back in the big apartment we grew up in, whenever one of us played the piano, you could feel the happiness in the air."

"You're right," my other sister replied. "As though the piano was happiness in a box . . ."

For once, they didn't seem to be making fun of anyone or anything. A hint of sorrow showed in their identical eyes.

So they had noticed, too. My sisters mustn't be as clueless as I thought. Our piano, now gone, was happiness in a box. The proof? Sometimes when I was little, my mom used to play bouncy music and sing along in her beautiful soprano voice. I'd sit under the piano with my giant panda bear. The vibration from the pedals and the felt hammers hitting the piano strings made my body quiver from the soles of my feet to the tips of my hair. I could feel myself floating.

The hill district

Where could I find happiness? Where could it be hiding in this city? That's where the piano would be. These thoughts went through my mind all week until today, Sunday, when I got up early. My mind is made up. I have to find our piano. In the bookcase next to the little gold Buddha, I find the city map, which I spread out on the living room rug. I study it.

Let's see. Happiness doesn't live in the poor district. Of that I'm positive. Happiness doesn't live in the business district either. And immigrants arrive with their own instruments, an accordion, a fiddle, a flute, or one of those funny African instruments made from a tin can and a few strings. So happiness doesn't rely on a piano in their district.

Then I decide. Happiness must be in the hill

district where the rich people live. I fold the map and carefully prepare the question I'll use as an introduction.

Now all that's left is to set out to look for the piano. I'm sure my father knows where it's hiding since he's the one who sold it. But I don't dare ask him, and anyway, he isn't home this Sunday. It must be a Sunday with the other woman. Actually, there's no talking at all anymore in the new apartment. I leave a note on the kitchen table for my mom saying I've gone to play soccer with some friends. I add three x's and sign my name.

I head toward the hills that border the city to the north. First, I head up an ugly four-lane boulevard sporting neon signs, pizza joints, and dancer bars. I turn off toward the winding streets lined with tall trees and single houses, all signs of a wealthier district.

Soon I reach the hills. I breathe deeply three times through my nose and ring the first doorbell. I begin, "Sir, excuse me for bothering you. Would you happen to have bought a grand piano recently

with a small scratch on the right-hand side and the word Steinway written on the front, just above the keyboard?"

"Of course not! How ridiculous!" the man says, shutting the door in my face.

Eleven houses later, I get a yes from a woman with a long, black braid who's wearing a frilled apron and a white bonnet. She has a Steinway in the living room. She even lets me inside to have a look, as long as I take off my shoes so I don't disturb the lady of the house, who's upstairs. I walk into the living room and see pictures on the walls of little cabins and forests with red autumn leaves. There are armchairs with legs in the shape of lion's paws, that look as if they're sleeping on the patterned rug. But the color of the Steinway, its top down, is mahogany. Our piano is black.

So I go on to the next house, then the next. A man with messy hair wearing a bowtie invites me in to see his harpsichord. I politely turn him down. I hate the sound of a harpsichord. It's not the sound of happiness, more a clinking sound.

Farther down, a woman whose blonde hair is pulled back with a bow wants to play the harp for me. I couldn't care less about harps or Christmas angels; that's not what I'm looking for.

The few pianos I do find in the houses in the hills all look lifeless.

As night falls, I head back down in the bitter cold toward the boulevard lined with bars, gas stations, and neon signs. I feel discouraged. My expedition to the hill district was a waste of time. My piano doesn't live there. Happiness doesn't always set up house in the homes of the very rich.

I also have a strange feeling—that I have no choice, that I have to keep looking. If I don't find the piano, a terrible thing will happen to someone.

That someone is my mom.

The cracked key

I think about the piano all week long. I study the city map and rack my brains trying to decide where to look next. My thoughts keep going round in circles. I wake up in the night worrying. My mom talks in her sleep, but I can't understand what she's saying.

While I lie there, I'm visited by images of the piano. When I was little and the great black wooden top was always open, I'd drag a chair over and climb up. I plucked one string, then another,

feeling the vibration in my arm, my head, and my stomach all at once. I could feel myself floating again, like the Tibetan monks who murmur "omm" and levitate. Honest. One of my sisters said so once. She also told me that Tibetan monks wear red robes.

When I wake up on Saturday morning, I'm struck by a brilliant idea. What I need is a piano tuner! Piano tuners criss-cross the whole city as they work on out-of-tune pianos. All I need to do is look in the phone book.

Under the heading "Piano Tuners" I find two listings. I punch in the numbers on the phone. I'm the detective of the century. The first tuner

has never come across a black Steinway with a scratch on the right-hand side. The second tuner doesn't stop for a second. "A Steinway? Made of black ebony? With a cracked ivory key?"

My heart races, panic-stricken. A cracked key? I'm not sure. But wait…yes! A tiny little crack… on a key just to the right of center. So I say almost in a whisper, "Oh! That's the one! Where is it?"

"With a piano teacher."

"Sir, I absolutely have to find it. It's a matter of life or death!"

He sounds amused, "Well, then, young lady, perhaps we should begin by arranging to meet."

He asks me to join him at the Polish Café on Sunday afternoon. That's in the neighborhood next to ours, the district of the artists and poor people.

I feel like hitting my mom

It's Sunday. I'm awakened early in the morning. In the kitchen, my mom is yelling and so is my father. Hurtful words. "Enough! You're completely crazy. I don't love you anymore!" He stomps out, slamming the door behind him. She locks herself in the bathroom. Later she takes refuge in her twin bed.

At noon, I open the fridge and grab the milk that I drink straight from the carton while stuffing myself with chocolate chip cookies. When I'm unhappy, I eat a ton of food. The apartment is as lonely as a cemetery.

Later, I leave a note on the kitchen table. "I'll be back in a while. I'm going to the park to roll around in the snow. Love and kisses." I sign my name.

I walk through the streets quickly, my cap

pulled down over my ears. Small wet snowflakes are falling, the first this winter, and storekeepers are decorating their windows with pine branches and colored lights.

The piano tuner is waiting for me outside the Polish Café. We sit in the booth next to the window and he treats me to a hot chocolate. He's wearing his tuning fork around his neck. It hangs from a bootlace like a jewel.

He seems curious to meet me. "It's a magnificent piano," he begins, "with quite an extraordinary sounding board. Did it belong to a musician?"

I tell him everything. The grand piano has been in my mom's family for generations. She inherited it from her grandmother and accompanied herself on the piano singing Mozart. My father fell in love with my mom during a recital.

"You don't say! I remember your mother!" the piano tuner exclaims, as he fingers his tuning fork. "Such a full, rich, yet fragile voice. I heard her give a concert a long time ago . . . Does she still sing?"

"Oh, no," I say. "Now she paints."

Then it all pours out of me. I tell him how, since the piano disappeared, no one loves anyone anymore and my grandma lives in a home, waiting to die, my father is never around, my sisters are mean, and my mom wanders from one room to another either carrying her paintbrush or sobbing with grief.

The only thing I don't tell him, because I'm ashamed, is that I, too, am mean now. I hate my crybaby nephews, I hate my sisters and their gossiping, and I'm furious with my father and that stupid woman. Sometimes at night, I feel like hitting my mom as she breathes too close, letting her unhappiness wash over me.

I tell him maybe the piano was the best part of us, and since the day it disappeared, it's as if dark shadows have crept in to live among us.

The piano tuner sees how serious this is. He'll speak to the piano teacher about me.

I'm sorry, Emily

I'm excited the whole week. My mom whimpers in her sleep. She's started painting again. This time she's tackled the moldings around the doors. She doesn't speak, or even eat much of anything other than sweet oranges from Morocco. My father hasn't come back since their last fight.

My two sisters come over on Wednesday evening without their screaming kids, just to see how we're getting along. They look worried. I can guess what's on their minds. They think our father won't ever come back to live in the apartment. So do I.

They tell each other that if this keeps up, decisions will have to be made. They shoot sideways glances my way. My sisters scare me. They're the type to make hasty decisions. I don't want my mom to be shut up in any kind of hospital. What about

me, will they ship me off to a boarding school?

The piano tuner calls on Saturday morning. "Go to this address on Sunday," he says. "At one p.m. sharp. Someone will be waiting at the door." He gives me the address and hangs up.

I rush over to the address he gave me, just to see. I don't need the map since the street is in the same area where the piano tuner lives. I run until I'm gasping for breath. On the boulevard, loud-speakers are broadcasting Christmas carols.

I stop in amazement in front of the stone building with its huge carved wooden front door. It's the convent for the nuns who run a soup kitchen for the poor. The nuns are very old. According to my sisters, they're an endangered species. There are hardly any nuns left in our city.

I look up at the big arched windows. I want to go inside right away and hunt down the piano. It's hard to have to wait a whole day. I hold myself back. It's getting colder by the minute. Finally, I clench my fists deep in my pockets, turn on my heel, and walk home.

In the evening, my father comes to the apartment carrying an empty suitcase. He takes his clothes out of the closet in the front bedroom and throws them any which way into the suitcase. My mom has shut herself in the bedroom with the twin beds.

My father tries to hold me in his arms. I struggle. I yell all kinds of mean things at him. "If you think she's crazy, why would you leave me alone with her?"

He slaps me.

Then he starts to cry and strokes my hair, murmuring, "I'm sorry, Emily."

He says children can't know how complicated and strange grown-ups' lives are, even to them. How sometimes life is like a canoe trip down a dangerous river when the canoe tips and sinks. How sometimes a person has to run away, or how …

What about me? Do grown-ups know what they're doing to me?

I levitate

Sunday again. Big, soft snowflakes are falling, the kind I like. Winter is here to stay. Another sweet note. "Mommy, I'm going to play Scrabble with my friends. I love you."

A very old woman dressed all in gray is waiting for me by the carved door. Her eyes are a dull

blue, and she's shivering from the cold. She says, "Welcome, Emily. Come in. I'm Sister Isabelle."

My heart is pounding and I don't dare ask about the piano or anything else. I follow her inside. We take a wide staircase up at least three flights of stairs. Sister Isabelle climbs lightly, as though her legs were younger than the rest of her. I breathe in the smell of beeswax from the floor and the creaking steps.

The staircase narrows. It feels as if we're making our way to the attic. I wonder how they carried the piano this far. I'm never around for moves, so who knows? No one ever explains anything to me.

Now we're in front of a dark wooden door. Sister Isabelle turns the key in the lock and opens the door wide. We enter a round room. A rotunda, I think. Huge windows look out over a garden blanketed in snow at the back of the convent. A muffled silence. Curtains as flimsy as veils on the windows. Dark hardwood floors. Smack in the center, like a king, an emperor, a god, sits the piano.

I draw near and my knees start to tremble slightly. I gently brush the scratch on its side as though it were an old scar. I breathe in the smell of the ivory keys. The grand piano top is open and I pluck a string. The vibration between my fingers runs up my hand and reaches my brain in waves. I whisper, "Please play."

Sister Isabelle sits down on the wooden bench. "I'll start with a lullaby," she says softly. "First, you need to be comforted, little Emily." I slide under the belly of the piano. I lie back and wait.

She begins. A lullaby turns into Mozart, followed by a lively dance, while I lie still underneath the piano. Soon, I start to levitate. I float, very slowly, just above the ground, and I'm the only one who can tell.

I picture again all the happiness the piano brought such a long time ago when my mom sang, "The Old Lamplighter," my sisters played duets, my parents sneaked stolen kisses, and we had a real live Christmas tree.

As the soft light from the snow begins to fade,

Sister Isabelle stops playing, leans over, and asks me how I feel. I smile.

"You can come back every Sunday," she adds. "If you like, you can bring your mother."

"Oh, yes," I say.

I come out from my hiding place and kiss her old wrinkled cheeks, then, just as I'm leaving, glance at the wall next to the door and see a small picture of a man with a shaved head wearing a red robe. He has glasses and is smiling: he must be one of those Tibetan monks. His eyes love me.

A big, fat tree

I've moved into the front bedroom. Now I'm the one who sleeps in my grandma's bed. My mom has started eating vegetable soup and rice cakes as well as oranges and has finished painting the doorframes. Now she's started on the baseboards. I actually like the look of the gold ribbon running along the floor and winding around the doors like a trail of light through the whole apartment.

Yesterday, we went to the market together and bought a big, fat Christmas tree. Coming back along the boulevard, I held the treetop and my mom the trunk, and we laughed. My mom painted the glass balls gold. I hung them from the tree with a set of little pointed lights and garlands. A papier-mâché angel plays the trumpet at the very top. We have come up with the most beautiful Christmas tree I've ever had.

My sisters dropped by a couple of times. They poked into everything and decided the house was clean and the fridge was full. They no longer talk about decisions or boarding schools or hospitals. My mom greets them warmly and kisses them on the forehead. I ignore them.

My father called and invited me to spend New Year's Eve with him and his woman friend. I said no. Maybe next year.

I've taken my mom to Sister Isabelle's rotunda several times now. The first time, I think she would have taken the piano in her arms and kissed each one of its ivory keys if she could have. But it's too fat. A grand piano is as big as an elephant. She sat down and played. She sang in a little, half-broken voice. She cried. She hugged Sister Isabelle to her and whispered, "Thank you, thank you."

The monk of the picture and I looked down on the two of them with hearts full of love.

The last Sunday

Today is both Christmas and a Sunday. Soon, after New Year's Day, my mom is going to start teaching piano in the rotunda. Sister Isabelle says she's getting old and that she'll give my mom her students. Everything is working out. The evil curse is tiptoeing out the door.

In a few minutes, we're leaving. First, we're going to take a poinsettia and some chocolate truffles to my grandma in the nursing home. Maybe I'll even give her a kiss.

Then we're going to the convent. The piano tuner is coming, too. We're going to share a meal in the big hall with the poorest of the poor, the people who don't have a home or a person to love anymore. Then we'll go up to the rotunda with anyone who feels like it and my mom will give a private recital. Her first recital in twenty years.

Oh! Here she comes. She's wearing the gold-threaded blouse she wore when she used to play piano and sing on stage. She's shining with light, just like the sun.